My Hot Wife - A Cuckold, Male Chastity, Female Led Relationship, Feminization Story

By Barbara Deloto and Thomas Newgen

To purchase another copy of this book or to see our

other books go to

http://www.ShapeShifterBook.com
Other books written by Barb and Tom
Shapeshifter
Changes: Erotic Tales of Forced Feminization
Changes II
Virgin Bride - An Erotic Tale - A Husband Becomes a Bride
Virgin Call Girl - An Erotic Tale - A Wife Turns Her Husband into A Call Girl
My Wife's Success - A Sissy Cuck Tale
Feminizing Men - A Guide for Males to Achieve Maximum Feminization
Feminizing Men - A Tale of a Husband's Forced Feminization by His Hot Wife
Bored Guys - A Couple of Bored Guys Get Cross Dressed and Turn into Fully Feminized, Sissy Faggot, Tranny Sluts.
The Hypnotist - A Cuckold Husband is Hypnotized and Turned into a Shemale
An Addicted Cross-Dresser, Married, and a Happy Ending - A True Story: A Book to Share

1

My name is Dan. At this moment, I'm sitting here with my chrome-plated, male chastity cage on, throbbing inside of it, enjoying the pleasure of knowing I'll continue to be aroused and my libido will continue to increase, until the time my love, my hot wife, Morgan, allows me to have my occasional reward.

I used to reward myself twice a day thinking about her. It wasn't as if we didn't have sex or anything. It's not that I didn't satisfy her either. We did it every night. She had to have it, as did I. I loved giving it to her. Then, I found out how to give her even more pleasure than I could myself. Now, we both have more pleasure in our daily lives than most people have in an entire lifetime.

How can that be, you ask? My male part is trapped inside of a metal cage, unable to have a full erection, and only allowed to have a reward on certain occasions instead of at least two or three times a day, and yet, my wife and I both have much more pleasure?

The thing that prevents other couples from achieving this is our societal beliefs and norms. What's accepted and what is taboo. If you evaluate those beliefs and taboos, you find that you can increase life's real rewards without hurting anyone, or taking drugs of any sort. Life's pleasures multiply and become greater, and the bond between a couple can grow - sometimes. In our case it did.

It all started with how much I loved my wife and wanted to provide her the best things in life. Little did I know what it would require.

2

We were on vacation at a beach resort. We lay on our stomachs and enjoyed the sun tanning us, as I smelled the coconut tanning oil on the salt air of the ocean breeze. Her long nails scratched my scalp as she rolled my head over to see her.

She looked into my eyes. "Dan, there are a lot of hot women here aren't there? See that one in the pink bathing suit behind me?"

I looked over her head and laid back down to gaze into her bright green eyes. "She's okay I guess. You're hotter." I ran my hands through her long, auburn-red hair as the sun glinted off of it.

"C'mon, you can't be serious. I mean, she's exotic."

"Your the most beautiful woman in the world to me. What about all the hot guys here? How about the one that's lying next to your hot woman? He looks nicely built, and handsome. Must be about six-foot-four."

"Yeah! He's hot all right. At least I can admit it."

"You should admit it. You're gorgeous and deserve to get hot for guys. I'll bet you could take him away from the woman he's with, since you're hotter than she is."

"I'm not and don't even think about something like that."

"Why not. Let's make a bet. We have all week here; we may as well make it interesting. Then I can prove to you that you're the hottest girl on the beach."

Morgan's eyes opened wide under her sunglasses and it raised her eyebrows above the frames. She shifted her pelvis against the blanket. I could tell the talk we were having was arousing her.

"So what would I do with the guy once I distracted him from his woman? When is it proof? And if I don't distract him from her, what do I win in this bet?" She ran her hands through my thick blond hair.

"I don't know. Details, details. I think it would be hot to see you flirt with him and see what happens anyway. I know you'd win him away from her. So, my reward will be seeing you win him over, proving my point that you're hotter. What should your reward be?"

"How about if I win him over, you don't ask me to do this again, and we enjoy our vacation? If I don't win him over, you bang me good."

"Hmm. I think I can do that. Then we have a deal?"

"Deal. Enough of this talk. I'm gonna take a swim."

Morgan rose from the blanket. Her yellow bikini was still wet between her legs from the last dip. That's odd, my

4

bathing suit was totally dry. My guess is hers was wet from our talk.

I sat up and watched her prance her perfect body across the sand and into the waves. I looked over to the two we were talking about. The woman was talking to him, and he was just staring off at the ocean watching my wife as she bent down to pick up a flat rock and skip it across the waves. He flashed a big smile and his girlfriend slapped him on his hard bicep.

Morgan dove into the water and swam out a ways and back again. She stood and started to walk out of the undertow. Her top was missing. It didn't come off any other time she swam in that top. She walked up the beach as if nothing had happened.

The guy took his sunglasses off for a better look. Morgan turned to face the ocean and look for her top. The fluorescent yellow of the top was obviously being flipped and flopped by the waves. She looked away from it as if she didn't see it.

The guy stood and ran down to save her. He dove into the waves and snatched up her top, swam it back to her, and stood towering before her with it. I could see Morgan thank him as she slipped it over her head, placed the cups on her perfect, hard-nippled breasts, and tied the halter. She pranced her way back to our blanket and flopped on her apple bottom.

She grabbed a towel and dried her hair. "I can't believe my top came off. I guess I didn't tie it right last time."

She laughed. "Yet, I took him away from his girlfriend, so I guess I'm done with that at least."

"Well that was just a damsel in distress technique. Any woman could have had him come help them like that. Sorry. You haven't proved my point yet."

She put her sunglasses back on. "Okay, you win then. I failed. You have to bang me good then." She kissed me on the lips. I could taste the salt water. Her hand slipped between us to my crotch. "Hmm, seems like you're ready."

I moved her hand away. "Yeah it was pretty hot watching you show that guy your gorgeous boobs. I need to get it to go down though, so we can eat lunch. You still need to prove he's not gonna jump your bones if he gets the chance."

"C'mon Dan. Jump my bones? Just bang me." Her nipples were poking up bumps in her bikini top. This was exciting to her regardless of what she was saying. She caressed her thigh with her hand.

I picked up my towel and folded it so I could carry it across my arm in front of me. "Let's go eat lunch."

I stood and took Morgan's hand. We walked to the bar and sat in the shade facing the beach.

"Two long island iced teas please," I said to the bartender.

Morgan said, "Long island iced tea? Are you trying to get me drunk?"

"It's vacation isn't it?"

Morgan's bathing suit saver sat down next to her, and his girlfriend next to him.

"Oh hi," he said to Morgan.

"Hi. Thanks again for the help. I don't know what I'd have done if you didn't find it."

"I don't think it would have been all bad. Glad I could help though. My name's Anthony. You can call me Tony." He shook her hand.

I stuck mine out to him. "I'm Dan. Thanks for the help."

"Nice to meet you, Dan. No problem," he said.

His girlfriend stuck her hand across and leaned over with her boobs on the bar. She was pretty. "I'm Jeana."

We shook her little hand and said hi.

Our long island iced teas arrived.

Tony commented, "Long island iced tea. What a great idea." He ordered two more. "So Dan, are you and Morgan married?"

"Yeah we are. Many years. You guys?"

"Nah. Just met this week."

"Here for the week?" Morgan asked.

"Till Sunday," he said.

I leaned across Morgan with my arm around her shoulders. "It's Morgan's birthday today."

Tony smiled at her. "Happy Birthday Morgan! We should celebrate."

The band started playing in the corner. I elbowed Morgan and whispered in her ear. "See, celebrate. Now prove me wrong by flirting with him. I want to see if he doesn't dump her for you. I'll bet he does."

She glared at me, sucked most of her drink down through the straw, put her hand on his hairy, muscled thigh, and looked him in the eye. "That's an excellent idea. How about if we start by dancing."

Tony looked at me. "Great idea. Go dance with Tony," I said.

Tony took her tiny hand in his huge one and led her to the dance floor under the patio cover. They started to dance. Morgan put her dirty dancing on for him and you could see he wanted her.

Jeana sucked down her long island iced tea, looking at them with disdain. She plunked it onto the bar. "I gotta headache. Tell Tony I left." She hopped off her seat and took off for the hotel.

Tony and Morgan came back. Morgan was brimming with excitement. Her nipples were hard as erasers under her top and Tony was showing something that was twice my size through his shorts.

"Thanks Tony that was fun." Morgan said as she put her hand in his lap and kissed him on the cheek. She took her hand back and looked at me questioningly. I smiled and nodded an okay to her to go ahead.

Tony sipped his drink and looked at me. "Dan, hope you didn't mine me dancing with your wife."

"Of course not. She loved it. I'll never stop her from having anything she wants."

"Wow. That's great. You must love her a lot."

"I do."

Morgan chimed in. "And I love Dan." She held my arm in both her hands and kissed me.

I took her hands off my arm and whispered in her ear, "I think you found someone to make love to you today."

She glared at me. "Shush! No!"

I whispered in her ear again. "At least see if he would. That's the bet."

She took a deep breath and rolled her eyes. She sucked down the rest of her long island iced tea and moved it to the edge of the bar for a refill. "It is vacation, so I think I'll have another."

Tony pointed to her drink when the bartender came over. "I'll get it, and get my man Dan one too, and I'll have another."

"Thanks Tony," Morgan said and she put her silky hand on his hairy thigh and slid it under the leg of his shorts. Tony looked at me.

I nodded and smiled. "Looks like that might be a better birthday present than a dance."

Morgan took her hand from him and glared at me. "Dan!"

"Why not? If it's okay with Tony."

Tony laughed. "Holy shit. How lucky can a guy get? You'd let me do that to your goddess of a wife?"

"Not let. Ask you to as a gift. I want to see her have a special week this week and that would make it special."

"Dan stop."

"What, Tony isn't handsome? Is he gross?"

"I don't even know him. It's you I love."

"This isn't about love. It's about sex - immensely good sex that you deserve. Right Tony?"

"Whatever you say boss. It'll be good, I promise. Haven't had any dissatisfied customers yet." He winked at Morgan, put his huge hand in her hair, and tugged it lightly. Morgan gasped and twitched then crossed her legs and started bouncing a foot.

"So you think you're that good?" Morgan asked as she put her hand back on his thigh and under his shorts.

"I know I am." He tugged her long hair lightly pulling her head back a little.

"Mmm," Morgan said. She took his hand from her hair and reached for her drink. She sucked it down. "Damn. These are the best long islands I've ever had. Phew."

Tony put his hand on her thigh and gently squeezed it. "You have gorgeous legs. They feel so nice."

"Thanks. And you're very handsome. And from what I can tell…" She slid her hand under the leg of his shorts and wrapped her fingers around his growing bulge. "…you have a pretty sizable tool too." She moved closer to him on her seat. He put his arm around her shoulders.

"Thanks. No woman has complained about it yet." He leaned in to kiss her and looked at me first. I nodded. He kissed her on the lips while holding her head by her hair. Morgan resisted at first then melted into his embrace. She rubbed him through his pants and made him grow even larger. She moaned as they kissed.

Tony pulled away from her and stroked her hair. Morgan's eyes were drooping a little. "Mmm, you're a good kesser." She was starting to slur. "You need to make love to me so my husband can win his bet and I can come. He has to come with us though."

Tony's eyes popped wide open and he looked at me.

"Let's do it," I said. "She needs it."

Tony looked around and found the men's room. "Okay, follow me." He threw a fifty under his drink and took

11

Morgan by the hand. I looked around as we entered and no one saw us go in.

My heart was racing just thinking about Morgan having this guy make her swoon. There were changing rooms with doors on them. Tony opened the door and held it for us. He closed it behind him and dropped his shorts. I took out my phone and started to make a video of them.

Morgan's eyes popped wide open as she looked at his huge rod throbbing in the air. She looked at me droopy eyed and I nodded my head for her to continue. She knelt down and took him in her mouth. Mine was hard as a tree as I watched my wife suck this guy, bobbing her head up and down while his hands gripped her hair and pushed himself deep into her throat. He took a Magnum rubber out of his pocket and opened it. He slipped out of her mouth and slipped the rubber on.

Morgan watched. "Yes, oh yes."

He slid his fingers under her bikini bottom, slid three fingers into her, and pumped her with his hand. She held onto his shoulders to steady herself as she whimpered quietly. She squirted on the floor as she came on his hand.

Tony wrapped his huge hands under her bottom and lifted her against the wall. Morgan reached for his magnificent tool and slid herself onto it. She whispered, "Oh my God Tony. It's fantastic. Take me like the whore I am."

Tony pinned her to the wall and rammed in and out of her. Morgan's eyes rolled back in her head as she held onto him with her legs wrapped around him and her arms around his neck. "God Tony, that feels so damn' good. More baby, more."

Watching and listening to Morgan enjoy herself like that was incredible. I held the phone with one hand and continued to record this momentous event while I stroked myself. Morgan hung onto him tight as she whimpered and he rammed her repeatedly. She pulled his hair with one hand. "Harder!"

Tony obliged and pounded her, taking that velvet hammer almost all the way out, and then he rammed it all the way in, faster than I'd ever seen anybody do, including myself. He was a machine.

Finally, Tony was ready. "Morgan baby I'm ready. Can you come with me?"

"Yes!"

Tony thrust even faster, clenching her tightly to his huge body as he jammed each spurt into his rubber deep inside her. Morgan's body tensed and jerked as she came with him. I spurted on the floor, my legs became weak, and I nearly fainted it was so intense.

They both relaxed. She ran her hands through his hair and looked dreamily into his eyes. He planted kisses on her forehead, cheeks, and lips. "Oh baby," he said as he thrust slowly and continued to kiss her.

Morgan said, "Oh my God, that was incredible."

She kissed him deeply on the lips holding his head to her.

She leaned back from him and looked dreamily at him.

"I very, very, much LOVED how you made me feel."

She kissed him deeply on the lips for quite a while as he continued to slowly stroke in and out of her. He leaked around the base of his sheath and it dripped down Morgan's leg, which was already wet from her.

They were beautiful. It was absolutely exquisite to see the pleasure Morgan had received and to hear her say so to her lover.

I stopped recording

In spite of the beauty and her joy, I felt remorse and my ego asked me how I could allow another man to make love to my wife.

3

Tony and I pieced Morgan back together and I took her back to our room. She fell on the bed and didn't wake up until evening.

Sitting on the couch in our room, I watched the recording on my phone over and over. I couldn't believe I let some guy make love to my wife. I was remorseful, but in spite of that, as I watched how much she enjoyed it in the recording, I knew I wanted her to have it whenever she desired. My emotions were mixed.

It seemed as soon as I had finished and experienced an orgasm better than any I had before, I started to feel weird - like I was a pervert for wanting to see my wife enjoy herself like that. Nonetheless, I never made her feel THAT good myself, and she deserved to have it - every twitch, every body convulsing reaction, every gush of pleasure.

Her hand touched my shoulder. "Is that of me? Dan, delete that!" She reached for the phone. I held it away from her.

"No. I want to keep it. I love seeing how enjoyable it was for you."

"You do?"

"Yes. I do. Wasn't it good for you?"

"Well, I was a little drunk, so it might have been better if I wasn't. Overall, it was okay." She sat on my lap.

"It was more than okay. I could tell. Don't feel bad. I liked seeing you enjoy yourself like that."

"You didn't feel jealous?"

"Just jealous I couldn't have done it that good. I did feel weird after I finished and spurted on the floor."

"You had an orgasm?"

"Well, I uh."

"While Tony and I were doing it?"

"Yup. Right when you both climaxed together at the end. When he emptied himself into you. It was so exciting I don't think I would even have had to touch myself. You two were incredible to watch. The way he made you feel. It was as if I was feeling your excitement and fulfillment."

"You enjoyed it that much huh? Well, I'm glad you enjoyed it."

"Yes I did. Immensely. Thanks for giving me that."

She laughed a little laugh. "No problem. So, you said he released in me!?"

"He had protection on. It wouldn't matter anyway. You can't get pregnant."

"I know that. We just don't know if he's clean or not."

"Understood. I think he is."

16

She nuzzled my neck. "It was pretty wild. I'm glad it's over though."

"Honey, we have all week."

"No. It's over."

It doesn't have to be. Tony said he's going to dinner in the hotel restaurant on the patio tonight. They have a band and it's a dress-up dinner."

"That sounds like fun. I can wear something pretty."

"Absolutely. I'm sure Tony would appreciate something sexy too. I know I would."

"Dan, no. I don't want you to feel weird. I want to make you happy."

"Don't worry about me. I'll be fine. If you're not too sore, I'd say we eat, have drinks, and come back here with Tony."

Morgan flattened her lips out and scrunched her eyes down in a scowl. "Dan!" She rolled her eyes and her head.

Instantly, she changed her look into a huge, excited smile. "I think I'll wear my super short, black sequin, V-neck, mini-dress with the five-inch strappy heels." She hopped off my lap anxious to get ready.

"I'll try to hurry, sweetie." She ran into the bathroom.

4

We spent the week hanging out with Tony and he made love to my wife at least twice a day. Every time I released while watching them though, I was overcome with the idea I was some kind of freak. Morgan noticed it a few times after the daytime sessions.

We returned home and into our normal routines. In the morning, and at lunch at work, I'd release myself while watching any of a number of videos of my wife and Tony. Then Morgan and I would do it every night before we fell asleep like usual. I realized how truly trivial the pleasure she received from me was compared to what Tony gave her, yet she said she didn't care.

"I love you Dan. I don't care how hard or how long I experience my climax, as long as we can do it together and you're happy. I don't like how you feel weird after I do it with someone else. You shouldn't feel weird. If you do, then we should stop."

"It's only after I release. It fades quickly."

"Does it happen after you release when you're watching the videos?"

"Yeah, about the same."

"Hmm. Maybe you shouldn't release anymore then, so you don't get that horrible feeling that is. Good night baby."

5

About a week later, a package arrived in the mail for Morgan. I put it in the pile with the rest of the mail and started making supper. By the time I was done cooking, Morgan was home. She looked gorgeous in her normal work-attire of heels and skirt-suit. Today her suit was black with light pink pinstripes. Her pink satin blouse was unbuttoned enough to see the edge of her pink pushup bra and her creamy cleavage.

She came around the counter and kissed me on the lips with her arms around my neck. "Hi baby. Have a good day?"

"Alright, I guess. There's a package for you on the counter."

She let me go me and stepped over to it. "Oh good! I bought you a gift. I hope it works." She hurriedly opened it sliding one of her long, painted nails under the flap. "Yes!"

She held it up in front of my face. "This will help you to not feel bad after."

I took it from her. It was a chrome cage with a little padlock on it. "How is this supposed to help?"

"It's a male chastity device honey. You put it on so you can't release until it's the right time."

I looked at the instructions. It didn't look like fun. "Why should I wear this?"

Morgan came over by me, took the cage, and ran her long nails across the cold steel. "I did some research on us. It seems we aren't the only couple that did what we did. This is supposed to be worn by you so you can increase your arousal and libido and not get the final reward until it's the proper time. That way, you won't feel remorseful. I thought you'd like to try it."

Evidently, Morgan was ready to do what we did again and she was trying to help me feel better about it. This was a good thing. "So if I put this thing on, when do I get the final reward, as you say?"

She stood straight and matter of factly said, "When I say you can." She giggled.

"Okay. When should we start?"

"Start now. Go put it on and I'll get dinner on the table."

I did as I was told. It seemed a mixed blessing. I was able to give my wife what she loved, and I loved seeing her receive, but I had to abstain from a final release until she allowed me that reward. It made sense though, and I was confident it would help me eliminate my unwanted emotions, which would enable me to continue providing the joy my wife so deserved to experience.

I struggled to get the ring around my globes and my meat through the ring. Then I pinched some of my skin trying to push the cage over it. I did get it on though and snapped the padlock shut. I was firm inside of it. It felt heavy and compressed it. It was quite stimulating. Then when I thought of wearing it when Morgan was stuffed with some nice big man meat, I filled it until my skin was squeezing from the slots.

I pulled my pants up, stuffed the keys in my pocket, and made my way downstairs. Morgan was finishing putting the drinks on the table. "That was quick!"

"I guess. It feels kinda good actually."

"Good." She held her hand out. "Keys please."

I dropped them in her hand and she put them on her chain around her neck like a trophy.

"Why are you wearing them around your neck?"

"People, who don't know what they are won't care, and people that do know will broaden our social circle."

She sat at the table and patted my placemat to tell me to sit.

I sat down and felt the hard steel between my legs tugging on me. I needed to figure out something for Morgan so she could continue with having new and exciting lovers. I sipped my wine.

"Honey, I think we should go on the swingers' websites to see what kind of guys are out there - tonight. Maybe we can find some regulars for you to enjoy."

"You think that would be a good idea. Okay. If it makes you feel good. Do you think you'll feel better now that I control your orgasms? We don't want you to feel remorse every time I'm made love to."

"I think it'll help."

What have I created here? Now my wife was helping me to achieve what I wanted her to have. I throbbed inside of my cage thinking about it. It felt incredibly good.

6

"Dan, did you find any candidates?" Morgan asked as I scrolled through the favorites I saved for her on the app on my phone.

"I think so. You'll have to put this app on your phone so you can check them out and send them messages if you want."

Morgan kissed me on the cheek as I sat at the dinner table with dinner ready for us.

"This saves so much time when you have dinner ready like this. I love it. Now we can relax and enjoy each other."

She sipped her wine and seated herself. Her high-heeled shoe slid against my leg. I throbbed in my cage. It's been only two days of abstinence so far; on the other hand, when I was used to releasing at least twice or three times a day, and Morgan was too, this abstinence was making me hornier than ever.

I was sure she was too, since I was useless to her with my cage on. I wondered if she'd ever take it off now. I looked at the keys on her necklace between her cleavage.

"Honey, can we take the cage off tonight? Chances are, you could use it tonight too. You haven't had sex in a couple of days."

"That's okay dear. If you aren't having any, than neither am I, and the longer we wait, the hotter we get right? What do they say? Absence makes the heart grow stronger?" She touched my hand and smiled as she bounced her foot under the table.

She played with her phone while we ate. "I have the app downloading now. How was work?"

"The same. You?"

"Good. I think someone at work knows what these keys are for." She shook the keys on the chain. "Bill laughed when he saw them and winked at me."

"Oh no. We can't have this stuff where you work."

"What's the difference? If they know what it is, then they must be discreet too, or they wouldn't know, right?"

I shrugged my shoulders and resumed eating.

She looked at her phone. "Apps done. What's the user name and password?"

I told her. She typed it in and found the favorites. "Oh he's hot, yes. And, wow, would you look at that? You picked out Billy too!" She laughed and flipped her long auburn-red hair over her shoulder as she blushed.

She tossed the phone down and returned to eating. She sipped her wine and looked at me with those gorgeous green eyes wide with delight. "Honey, if you can do the dishes and clean up, I can go through the favorites and send out some messages to these guys after we eat."

"Of course. Good idea."

"And can you throw some laundry in too? The hamper's getting full."

"Of course."

Morgan ate and read on her phone. When we finished eating, I took her plate and glass into the kitchen with mine and started to do the dishes.

Morgan yelled from the dining room. "Honey, it would be good if you could clean the bathrooms and vacuum the house a little too. That will save us time later this week."

"Okay dear."

I did my tasks. I could feel the cage pull on me, yet with all the diversion in the work, there was no pleasure. I did take pride that I was giving my wife what she needed and wanted. Just like any good husband should.

When I was done, Morgan was already asleep.

7

The next day, we drove to work and came home as usual. I was used to wearing the cage now, although I missed the relief I used to get at least twice a day. I was hornier than I'd ever been and had to find something to get rewarded for soon.

Morgan kissed my cheek. "Honey, dinner is ready and the house is so clean. Thank you. Were you planning on folding the clothes and putting them away tonight?"

"Of course dear. I thought maybe we could take the cage off tonight and have some fun."

"Oh there's nothing more that I'd like to do than that, Dan. The way you've been cleaning and cooking and taking care of things around here, you certainly deserve it. I'd love to have you pump me a couple of times and finish inside of me while we're locked in each others arms."

"Oh honey that makes me so happy. I can't wait. Super! Yeah!" I banged the table with my fist and crossed my legs feeling my excitement grow in the cage. It was pleasantly hurting at this point. I put my hand on hers and looked into her eyes admiring her beauty. "Thanks so much honey."

"However my dear, we have to be good so we enjoy it more later, right?" She smiled and bounced her leg under the table. She unbuttoned her blouse a little so I could see her cleavage. I shrunk in my cage.

"Right, dear. You're right. Just how much longer do we have to wait?"

"Until Saturday that's all."

"Why Saturday?"

"Because that's when one of the men from the swingers club is coming over."

"Coming over? We didn't even meet him yet."

"I did. He met me for lunch today. He's very handsome and quiet tall too. I think you'll like him."

Wow. She was moving on this. I guess that was good and I'm glad she met him in a public place before inviting him over here. She's no dummy.

"So Saturday you'll need to help me get things ready if you can."

"Of course dear. Do you have a time he's arriving and food I should prepare?"

"I sent you an email with his likes and dislikes already. I'll need to get some new clothes, so I'm going shopping for them tonight. You do want me to look incredibly hot for him, right?"

I throbbed in my cage. "Of course. Maybe I can go shopping with you."

"Honey, with you there, I'd feel embarrassed trying on the types of clothes I'm buying. I'm going for a blatantly sexual look and don't want people thinking a conservative married couple like us has a wife like me dressing that way."

"Okay. SO, what should I do?"

"I think you should cruise the web and look at porn. Look up hot wives and cuckolding. I think you'll like that."

"Well, that will just make me hornier."

"Well, of course, silly." She laughed. "All the better for the future right?"

8

The weekend arrived faster than I thought. Saturday I drove to the grocery store, the liquor store, tobacco shop for cigars, and the florist - Morgan wanted fresh flowers by the bed and on the dining room table. I washed and waxed her car - she needed it done and didn't have time.

When I had everything ready and set up, Morgan asked me to give her a bath, loofa her, and scrub her calluses off her feet.

I did and loved the thought of getting her ready like she was a virgin for an offering to the gods of sex. It further aroused her having her body touched like that.

"Dan, this feels heavenly. Thank you for being such a wonderful husband. I'm the luckiest girl on earth." She kissed my forehead as I scrubbed her thighs while she sat in the tub. I stirred in the cage.

"Thanks honey. I'm glad you like this. I do too."

"After the bath, will you paint my toenails and fingernails? I could use a fresh coat."

"Of course dear."

I loved painting her nails. She was so sexy and her nails were a part of it. I took great care in applying it perfectly and put a topcoat of clear on after.

Then it was time for her to dress. I entered the bedroom and she handed me her bra. "Here, you can help. I think you'll like that."

"Of course."

I helped her with her bra. A shelf bra that left her nipples exposed. They were hard as erasers standing at attention. She handed me a black satin and lace garter belt. I wrapped it around her tiny waist and adjusted it. She handed me a sheer black stocking. I rolled it up and slid it over her painted toes, up her thigh, and attached the garters to it. I did the same with the other stocking, all the time swelling in my cage.

Next, she handed me a pair of crotchless panties in black lace and satin. I oriented them, slid them up her legs, and onto her shaved crotch. I adjusted them so her moist pinkness poked out.

Morgan said, "I probably should wear regular panties, since I'm already dripping, still, these are hotter aren't they? I mean, hotter for him to see me down there all wet and ready for him, right? What's a little dripping going to hurt?"

My cage was constricting my growth severely now. It felt wonderful.

"Undoubtedly dear."

She handed me her new high heels. The heels had to be almost as high as a dollar bill is long. I slid her tiny foot into them and strapped the three straps around her ankle. My artwork on her toenails showed proudly through the straps over her toes. I leaked some cream from the cage in my pants. I put on her other shoe.

She stood, picked up her dress from the bed, and slid it over her head. It was a black satin and lace mini dress with a low cut V-neck and sheer fabric over the breasts so her nipples showed under it. I zipped it up her back. The skirt was short enough so that the tops of her stockings showed. She was gorgeous! To think I was dressing her up so a hot guy could make love to her in front of me. Wow, I was thrilled.

"Do I look hot enough honey?" Morgan looked at herself in the mirror. "Good thing I don't have to run through the mall in these shoes. Thank God, they'll spend most of their time behind my ears. They're five-and-a-half-inches tall."

She practiced walking in them. They made her hips sway and made her take tiny steps. She was seductive as hell in them.

"You look extremely hot. Those shoes are incredible. I love what they do to your walk. He'll catch you if you try to run away in those, so I hope you like him."

"Oh I like him. He's hotter than Tony was."

She handed me a necklace and I clasped it behind her neck. It was a gold phallus and fell between her breasts

"Nice necklace honey."

"Thanks. Here are the matching earrings." She handed them to me.

I put them in her ears. I took the rest of her jewelry - her wrist bracelets, ankle bracelets, rings, and the wedding ring I gave her years ago - and adorned her with all of it.

She looked in the mirror. She handed me her hairbrush. "Up or down?"

"Down."

"I agree. I want him to be able to tug on it hard."

I brushed her auburn-red hair out until it was smooth and shiny. She fastened her hair in a ponytail, low on one side, and the tail draped over her right shoulder. She looked to be a goddess. She sprayed perfume on her breasts, legs, and hair.

"Is that a new scent?"

"You noticed. Yes, it's a pheromone perfume called Maximum Attraction. Smell good?"

"I think he'll love it."

"Good. I wanted to have a scent he'd remember me by."

Morgan felt her nipple against the sheer fabric of her dress. "This fabric feels so nice against my nipples. I can't wait for my lover tonight. I'm so horney!" She laughed.

Morgan turned and observed herself in the mirror on the door again. "I think I'm good to go." She looked at the clock on the nightstand. "He should be here in a few minutes." She kissed my forehead. "Thanks for getting everything done and helping me today. You're such a dream. Now, do you want to hide in the closet? We'll be eating dinner downstairs though, so you don't need to do it yet."

"Hide in the closet?"

"Oh, didn't I tell you? I'm sorry. Not many guys want to have sex with a married woman in front of their husband. It's too threatening to them in case you were to get jealous or something. Even if you're wearing a cage on your male parts, they still get nervous."

"I wouldn't hurt them."

"I guess others have had bad experiences. Some men change their minds after a hot guy makes love to his wife and makes her happier than he ever did. They get jealous and angry."

"I guess I could see that happening. Now what?"

"I don't want you to leave, because I only met this guy once, even though he seems okay. You decide dear. For the future, we'll have to figure something out so my men don't feel threatened by you. For tonight, well, I'd like you to hide."

9

I stayed upstairs. I heard Morgan meet him at the front door, and from the upstairs landing, I peeked downstairs. I saw her take him in and close the door then immediately drop to her knees, unzip him, and take him in her mouth. She consumed it like a prisoner that just came off a hunger strike.

She hadn't done that for me in years, but I knew why. She wanted him to last longer when he made love to her. For me, she didn't want to make me have to wait so long to release and work so hard at it. She's so thoughtful of me. That way I could just have her release once, or sometimes not, and I'd finish immediately.

He took it like a real man and waited patiently until she obtained her reward in her mouth, down her chin, and on her breasts. When she gagged trying to swallow it all, he popped loose, and spurted a thick load in her hair.

He stood her up and kissed her deeply on the lips as he ran his hand through her hair and embedded his cream into it like hair gel.

She leaned back and looked dreamily in his eyes. "Everything is ready. I have your favorite things. I hope you have a good time. I know so far I like what I've seen, and consumed. Mmm"

"So far so good Morgan. This was a nice way to kick the night off. I'm thirsty and hungry. Can you get me something?" He slapped her bottom. I could sense tension in her shoulders. Morgan didn't like to be told what to do or to be treated like a subservient woman.

"Of course, my prince."

She tottered off in her minced steps, clicking her way into the kitchen while he walked into the great room and started looking around. She came tottering back, her boobs bouncing, and her nipples as hard as ever showing through the sheer fabric. She carried a tray with the appetizers I made today and drinks that I prepared and put in pitchers in the refrigerator.

"Wow. You're fast, girl. Thanks." He took his drink and slugged it down. Before she placed the tray on the coffee table, he put his empty drink on it. "That was good. I'll take another, if you don't mind."

Morgan took the glass and ran off to the kitchen. He kicked his shoes off and put his feet on the couch. "Where would she sit?"

She came back in and looked confused. He pushed the coffee table to the side and patted the floor for her. "This would be a good place for you so we could chat."

She hesitated then sat daintily on the floor and sipped her drink. He put his hand on her head and stroked it, patting her like a dog. "Yeah. Real nice place here."

"Thanks."

"Nice appetizers too." He grabbed three, placing them on his palm. "Must have taken some time to make these."

"Yes, it did."

"You're a hell of a woman. This house is so well kept too. No dust. So clean. You can tell a hell of a woman lives here."

"Yes she does. Come to think of it, she sure is one hell of a woman. Thank you for pointing that out."

He was still petting her like a dog while she sat on the floor beside the couch. She pounded her drink down, stood up, and took his hand. "Come with me."

She led him to the door, opened it, and showed him the way out. "Sorry, Can't do this. I should have known when you patted the hostess on the ass in the restaurant at lunch this week. I don't like sitting on the floor and being petted like a dog. Thanks for the protein shake."

He looked at her with shock on his face. "But, what about…"

"Forget it. We're done. Have a good night."

She held the door looking fierce in her black outfit and heels with her auburn-red hair glistening and her phallus jewelry reflecting the light.

He shrugged his shoulders and patted her ass. "Your loss baby. Sorry you didn't work out." He ran his hand through his hair and stepped out the door.

Morgan snapped the lock shut behind him. She looked upstairs. "Dan, come down here sweetie. We have lots of food and drinks, and even cigars if you want one."

I came down the stairs feeling bad for her. I held her beautiful face in my hands. I wiped some of his juice off her dress with my thumb. "I feel so bad for you. Sorry this guy turned out like that."

"Shit happens, honey. I'm done with this stuff. I don't want any more strange men. He treated me like a piece of meat."

"Yes, he did." I stroked her hair. "He was a typical, patriarchal, macho male - a real jerk. He didn't deserve you no matter how nice what he had between his legs was. What do you say we have some drinks and appetizers? I'd hate to waste all of my preparations."

"I'm so sorry honey." Morgan said. "I hope I haven't disappointed you." She looked at me with teary green eyes.

"No Morgan. You made me proud. You're a powerful, intelligent woman and I'm glad you stood up for yourself. Now, go sit in the living room and I'll bring you appetizers and drinks and then cook you dinner, my goddess."

We did. It was great. My hot wife was as hot as ever and we ended the night in the bedroom with the keys to my cage. Morgan had a hard time getting the lock to open, and I was so excited after all the time I hadn't released, that I flooded inside the cage and on myself before it was unlocked.

"Sorry Morgan. I so wanted to satisfy you tonight."

She laughed. "I'm happy you spurted though. It was so cute! You deserved that reward too. I'll just plug my big vibrator into the wall and I'll be all set. It's what's been keeping me from going crazy all this time."

"You've been using that?"

"When you're in the shower I have. It takes the edge off by having orgasms with it. Women aren't like men – we need to release, despite that, it doesn't mean we're done. If I didn't release, I'd be a raging bitch, not a wonderful little subservient schoolgirl like you are in your cage."

She patted my head like a proud schoolteacher and it made me feel honored that she thought of me so fondly.

Morgan kissed my forehead and patted my head again. "You're a delight darling, but that guy tonight totally ticked me off the way he was treating me, so I think we can call this game quits. I don't think it's worth it."

"But Morgan. Think about how good it was with Tony. I'm sure there are many more like him out there."

"Maybe, maybe not. Nevertheless, I don't want you hiding when and if they come over either. Especially after all the work you do to get things ready for my lovers. It's not fair to you."

She shook her head and looked at me with those green eyes. She stroked my hair and her eyes popped open. "Hey, wait, that moron said what a good woman I was with the clean house and appetizers and such. I know how you can be nonthreatening and then you can be with us, if I ever do this again. I'm kind of getting excited thinking about it though, so I need to take care of that and then we need to sleep. Let me sleep on it and we can talk about it all tomorrow. I may have a solution my special pet. Don't worry your pretty head."

10

It was Sunday morning and Morgan was in her fuzzy leopard robe and slippers sipping coffee at the kitchen table. Her mussed hair glistened in the sunlight pouring through the window. She looked up at me as I entered.

"Hi sweetheart. Sleep good?"

"Slept great. You don't know how good it felt to relieve all that pent up arousal, even if the cage never came off."

"Good. You deserved that. Well deserved. You're such a good husband. I could never ask for a better one."

"Would you?"

"Would I what?"

"Ask if you could. For a better husband."

"Absolutely not! Why would you ask that?'

"Well, I wasn't very satisfying for you last night."

"Oh come now, Danny. Stop that. I love you. I loved seeing how excited you were even though I couldn't even get the cage off of you. I'm the disappointment. I sent that gorgeous piece of man meat home! I should have just sucked it up so you could watch."

"I don't ever want you to suck it up. If it's not good, shut it down, exactly like you did."

"Well, I don't want my husband hiding in the closet anymore. If this is to work, we need to make some changes so that you can be with me and enjoy my pleasure with me."

"I'm ready sweetie. Whatever you think will help. I'll do anything for you to give you this gift."

Morgan sipped her coffee and studied me. She reached over and pushed my hair off my forehead. She grabbed my chin and turned my head side to side. "This might work. You might even like it. In fact, I'm sure you'll like it. I think you'll be hot."

"What, like what? I said I'd do anything for you."

"Anything?"

"Yes. I love you and want to provide everything you possibly want. That's a man's job isn't it? To provide for his wife? I want to give you ultimate bliss and I don't care what I have to do."

"You don't care? Are you sure? I think you're willing, but this is big."

"Cutting off my nose big? Plastic surgery big? If it was, and I don't know why you looked at me like that, and turned my head to look at my face, but whatever it is, I'm in."

"Okay then. I already put a book on your Kindle app on your phone this morning."

I opened the app. The file downloaded and a picture of the cover popped up - "Feminizing Men - A Guide for Males to Achieve Maximum Feminization." I looked at Morgan with my mouth open. Secretly, I was experiencing excitement. I'd thought of doing that from time to time, although I never had the nerve. I thought Morgan would think less of me if I did and that it was just wrong for men to do.

She smiled and nodded her head. "Don't look so shocked my pretty pet. You don't have to do this if you don't want to. When he said how great a woman I was, I realized it was you, who do all of the work around the house, and you who always keep it perfect. You've been doing laundry and making meals and being the perfect mate. I don't mean to degrade you at all, rather I compliment you on your impeccable service."

"Well, thanks I guess."

"That made me think about you being a woman. If you presented yourself as a feminized male, there would be no threat to ANY men I might have over. Yet, you'd be here if I needed you. And, you'd be able to be upfront and personal when I was being made love to."

My heart raced. My face blushed hot. I expanded inside my cage, which I now filled with my expanding flesh as I thought about how to make it possible for Morgan. About giving her ultimate bliss and yet being there to witness her being made love to.

I took a deep breath. "I'll start today."

"Aw that's wonderful sweetie? You'd do that for me? You're an angel!"

"I told you. Anything. Do you think I'd look okay? You said I'd be hot."

She leaned toward me, grabbed my cage, and shook it. "I think you'll be a doll."

I couldn't help think how ridiculous this was, yet it enticed me to face the challenge. If I could do it well, Morgan can have bliss and I could see what it was that made me excited to think of being feminized. Who cares? So what? Why not?

"A doll. That would be great. Thanks. I think. Will you help?"

"I read that whole book already. If you hurry and eat breakfast and epilate your whole body, we can go to the mall and get you dressed and made up to see how you look tonight. You can read the book at night before we go to sleep or whenever. In any case, you must read it as soon as possible. It's short and to the point. I think you'll be perfect, like you are at everything. A perfectionist. I'm getting a little wet thinking of you like that - my husband as a pretty girl all sweet smelling and feminine. Mmm."

She kissed my forehead. "My princess."

"Epilate?"

"Yes, you can use mine for now. It rips the hair out by the roots so they don't grow back stubby. After a while, the amount of hair thins on your body as well, which is much more feminine. If you're man enough to rip all your hair out, that is. It will hurt."

I stared at her and saw genuine excitement on her face. I had to do it. I ate breakfast and 'epilated' my whole body. After all the pain, my body felt especially erotic. After I soothed the initial irritation, my skin felt silky and smooth, and the cage pulling on me intensified the erotic feel of it all.

Was I on my way to becoming a nonthreatening, feminized male, so my wife could be made love to by real men while I watched? Hmm. I continued to throb in my cage. I had no reservations at this point and felt we had achieved a breakthrough that would benefit us both for a long time to come.

I just needed to put aside my masculine ego for a while and suck it up. Right? I mean, she deserved it, and I wouldn't be a man if I didn't get her what she deserved.

11

My wife led me by the hand into the Victoria Secret shop. She walked straight up to a young woman in the back.

"My husband needs to honor a bet he lost at work and has to present himself as a woman in front of his whole organization. Naturally, he needs a bra, oh, and breasts," Morgan said.

The woman's eyes popped open then she quickly composed herself. She looked at me. "Risky bet eh?"

"No big deal. You wager and you either win or lose. I lost. I can pay," I said.

"Now that's a real man talking. I'll bet your wife just loves you." She smiled at Morgan.

"I do!"

"Okay, let me take some measurements. Come into the changing room so we don't embarrass you." She took me by the arm. Morgan followed.

We walked in the mall from there to a shoe store then to multiple women's clothing stores and a makeup and perfume shop. On the way home, Morgan made a detour to an adult bookstore and had me wait in the car. "Girl toys sweetie. You'd just be embarrassed. I need some new toys."

How awful. My wife had to get new sex toys, because I had to wear a cage and she didn't have any real sex anymore. I had to do well with this so she could have a woman's unsurpassed, impeccably perfect, sex life. I sat there and felt diminished by her purchase, yet even more determined to do what she asked me to do and fulfill my responsibility as a man to provide for her. I read the book on my Kindle app on my phone while she was inside.

Morgan came out with a bag of toys and drove us home. When we arrived, she sent me to the bathroom to rinse off while she picked out clothes for me and laid them on the bed.

When I finished showering, in the bedroom was Morgan waiting to help me dress, like I dressed her for her date night with the moron. She looked gorgeous, wearing the same outfit she had on that night. I felt like a king. Actually, a queen I guess.

She smoothed a scented body lotion over me then spritzed me with perfume. My cage was full and told me how good this was. My male ego was nowhere around. She slid the silky stockings up my legs and they felt like heaven had surrounded my legs. I was sure I'd break the bonds on my cage at that point. I dripped from it and Morgan noticed.

"Hmm. Seems you like this. This could be good for you."

My hands shook with excitement as she helped me dress in an outfit similar to hers. I was infatuated with it all. As if I had been enchanted. I had never been so electrified in my life. All my senses seemed to be heightened and the room seemed so bright it would blind me.

The shoes felt incredible to walk in - completely sexy and sensuous. It was as if I had genuinely become a woman in them the way they changed my posture and walk and how that felt.

I didn't feel the least bit male other than knowing that inside of my cage was a male-like THING, which couldn't do what normal male's parts did, because it was held in bondage. It was proper and fitting to be stunted inside of it. The cage made it appropriate to wear my attire and my attire made it appropriate to wear the cage. I was in perfect balance.

She took me by the hand to the bathroom and applied my makeup. I watched my face turn from me into some hot woman. It was astounding. She styled my long blond hair and curled it. It draped gracefully just above my shoulders.

"We'll get it cut into a shag. That'll be more fun for this and still be okay when you want to masquerade as a real man."

I looked at her playing with my hair and had to agree with her. Even with the 'masquerading as a real man.' Would I ever feel comfortable dressed as a man again? This felt too special to ever give up.

I was sure the cage would burst at this point and hoped it didn't, since it felt so darn good. This was better than sex. It was continual and long lasting, not short and then done. I knew this was like a long foreplay that would last forever, as long as I didn't finish. Yet, I so wanted to finish.

Morgan checked me out turning me this way and that. "You are hot! You may be hotter than I am. My gosh! You should have done this a long time ago."

I looked in the full-length mirror and I was hot. Hotter than I'd ever thought I could be.

We ate dinner and had a few drinks. I relished my new sensations. The pull of the breast forms on my chest with the cleavage they gave me, the sensual silkiness of the stockings on my smooth hairless skin, the pull of the garter belts on them as I walked, the walk I had as a result of the shoes. It was otherworldly.

Morgan touched my hand. "We'll need to get you some glue-on nails. Sorry I forgot that, and I didn't paint your toenails. You'll have to take care of that some other time."

I looked at her hands and at mine and she was right. The nails would help. I swelled in my cage thinking of having them. The dinner I made tasted especially good tonight. The flavors were so full and rich. Was it my preparation or was it me?

"Morgan, how's the food? It seems to taste better somehow."

"The crab legs seem like usual to me. They're good. You can't really prepare them any better, but they taste like normal." She sipped her wine and looked at me.

I sipped mine and was careful to line up my lipstick mark on the crystal with my lips. The wine even tasted fuller and richer.

"I don't know. Everything seems more intense - food, the smell of the perfume, the sensations on my skin. All of it."

"I think it must be the new you. It seems to stimulate your endorphins. I did notice your pupils were a little dilated when I did your eye makeup and that's from the endorphins. That's good. Another plus to your feminization to make it more exciting for you."

I uncrossed my legs beneath the table and recrossed them enjoying the sensation. "I never though this would be this good."

"Well I think you deserve a reward tonight. I think you should release somehow. You've been such a good girl Daniella."

"Daniella? Why not? And I'd oh so love to finish tonight."

"Then you clean up the dishes and we'll set to work on your reward when you're done."

I ate the rest of my meal hurriedly and had to wait for my wife to finish hers. She was laughing at me I was so excited. I made Morgan a drink and settled her on the sofa. She wanted her legs massaged before I did the dishes, so I caressed and massaged her gorgeous stockinged covered legs, all the while dreaming about release.

"Your legs are so sexy. They feel wonderful in these stockings."

"I'm glad you like them. The massage feels great. Why don't you go finish the dishes and come back and I'll massage your legs."

I hoped up nearly knocking her off the couch and ran into the kitchen in my heels. I scrambled around and finished cleaning it all up. I set everything up for breakfast tomorrow so Morgan wouldn't have to do anything except heat it up and eat.

I redid my lipstick, and sprayed on some fresh perfume. I made drinks for us both and sat on the couch next to Morgan.

"Lift those sexy legs up here and I'll massage them."

I put them across her thighs and she caressed and massaged them to my delight. She slid her hand under the hem of my dress and shook my full and tight cage.

"Ungh, God. Oh shit," I whimpered. My whole body shuddered and shook.

I gushed huge amounts of semen out of the cage, all over my dress and collapsed against the back of the sofa.

Morgan collected up the mess with her fingers and licked some of it off. She held the rest of the gooey, dripping cream for me to lick. I cleaned her fingers off. It was salty and thick and a bright pearlescent white. "That's a good girl Daniella. Clean up your reward. You certainly had a lot of it. How do you feel?"

I felt the wet stickiness inside of my cage and on my legs. I had the taste of my juices in my mouth. I sat up straight-backed and brought my legs together then pulled my dress down over them, trying to feel respectable. I sipped my drink.

"Are you okay Daniella?"

I looked into those gorgeous green eyes full of concern.

"Uh, yeah, I'm okay."

"What's the matter sweetie? I thought the reward would feel good?"

"Well, it did. It was the most satisfying finish I'd ever had. It had been so long, and the arousal had been so continuous, it was incredible. Except now, I felt like I fell off a cliff. Now, I didn't feel sexy, or feminine. Instead, I felt like a freak in a dress."

"Oh sweetie. I'm so sorry. I guess that was my fault. Now you're feeling remorse like before you had the cage and I had Tony. I don't want you to feel bad. I'm so sorry. You're dealing with society's norms and taboos. You know. Concepts like real men are men, don't dress and act like women, and real men don't share their wives and those sorts of paradigms.

I should have realized this would be like that for you." She ran her hand through my hair and kissed my cheek.

"It's not your fault. I need to get my emotions under control. I know how good this felt just minutes ago and I'm no different now, so I need to deal with it."

"Oh no. I don't want you to feel this way again. We'll have to find a way you can release that doesn't cause this. For now, we'll just have to hold you off so you can enjoy being feminized and nonthreatening. It'll be better for you that way. I promise."

"Why don't I go get back into male mode? It won't feel like a masquerade now."

"Being a male will feel like a masquerade refreshingly soon again, if you stay feminized and in your cage. All those wonderful feelings will return to you. Honey, you know you need to be feminized to be nonthreatening. You need to practice being a woman for this weekend."

"This weekend?"

"Yes dear. While you cleaned up, I messaged some more candidates. You're right. I know there are better men out there than the moron that came over. I'll be interviewing them this week and if you want to be here and not hide, you need to be feminized and pretty."

I stared at her. I knew it was society's taboos I was dealing with. Useless paradigms. Male ego. I had to overcome all of it. It was the only way I could enjoy seeing her in bliss this weekend. I so wanted her to be happy and satisfied. She had done so much work for me to be able to have me there with her. I had to get over feeling stupid and do what she said. Nonetheless, right then, I just wanted to put on my guy sweats and top I normally wore to bed..

"Is it okay if I get dressed for bed?"

"Of course sweetie. Go ahead. You get comfortable. Just leave all of the underthings on and put on your cute black baby-doll over it. Leave your heels on to come back downstairs too. You'll feel better that way in a little while. The good feelings will return quickly. You'll see."

"Of course dear."

12

I did feel better in a while and on Monday morning; I was again taken by the lure of my feminization. I woke up with a full cage and my nightclothes felt luscious against my smooth skin. I showered and put on a black satin robe, black thigh highs, and my bra and gel inserts, and slipped into a pair of black high-heeled mules. Morgan was right. I was completely enamored with being feminized again.

"Hi sweetie," she called from her seat at the table. "Thanks for getting everything ready for breakfast. You look stunning by the way. Your makeup is a bit off though. Maybe you should get up a while before me, so you can look your best at breakfast."

"Morgan, I have to shower and change for work after. Why get all dolled up?"

"I guess. Maybe just touch it up a little before you come down. After work, you can put it all back on. Don't worry if you can't have dinner ready when I get home. I'll understand."

"Thanks."

"How do you feel? Feel good being feminized again?"

I nodded as I ate my cereal. "Yes, it's wonderful."

"Good."

We ate breakfast and I read my book on my phone while we did. It reminded me I needed to get nails and it had some good ideas for decorating my cage that sounded cute, so I needed to get some ribbons and flowers.

"I'm going to get nails, ribbons, and flowers at lunch today. Anything else you want?"

"That'll be good. Just get anything that helps you feel pretty. Is the book good?"

"It's awesome! It has so many good things in it and I want to do every one of them."

I noticed how I held my spoon and glass and corrected it based on what the book had said. "It helps to remind me of all the aspects that go into femininity. I want to be the best for you."

"I know you do. You're always great at anything you do."

Morgan stood and put her dishes in the dishwasher.

I stopped reading when I heard her. "I'll finish cleaning up. Go get ready for work."

"Okay sweetie. I'll put some clothes out for you to wear to work."

"Thanks."

I cleaned up the kitchen, sprayed and wiped the counters, stove and table, and started the dishwasher. I hung the clean sign on it so I'd remember to empty it after I was dressed for dinner tonight.

Morgan was done showering so I hopped right in, washed off my makeup, and cleaned my cage, rinsing it well. My hairless body felt nice with the slick soap on it. When I entered the bedroom, Morgan had my things laid out on the bed.

"I have to wear these to work?" I held a pair of sheer pantyhose and a bra without padding or inserts.

"Of course dear. It will help you feel less masculine and remind you of your goals."

"I guess."

I slid the pantyhose on and it did feel good. Morgan already cut the crotch out so I could poke my cage though it. The bra felt good the way it compressed me and lifted my pecks. I had to tell myself not to feel silly. This was important and it was just old paradigms and my ego making me feel silly.

I finished dressing and made the bed. Picked up Morgan's dirty clothes off the floor and threw them in the laundry basket. I left it out so I'd remember to run a load before I left for work. I picked out a dress for myself for tonight and matched underthings and jewelry.

I realized I should probably take a half-day vacation in order to buy nails and do them as well. I wanted painted toenails and nice long painted fingernails tonight.

I yelled to Morgan as I took the laundry basket downstairs. "I'm taking a half day vacation today so I can do my nails and have dinner ready when you get home honey."

"Oh how nice. Wonderful! I can't wait to see you."

The week flew past. Morgan was right, as usual, about wearing things under my man clothes at work. It helped me to gain confidence in what I was doing and helped me to feel sensual all day. The women's clothing under my work clothes did help me to feel that me being a real man was just a masquerade, which ultimately made me feel more at home when I was fully feminized after work, since I wasn't a man anymore.

Every night we'd enjoy each other on the couch just touching and caressing each other's legs and kissing carefully so as not to mess up our lipstick.

I had become pretty good at doing my own makeup, hair, and dressing, and Morgan said she ordered a very feminine surprise for me to wear this weekend. She made a hair appointment for me to have mine cut into a shag on Saturday morning.

I was once again continuously on the edge in my cage and looked forward with excitement to Saturday night so Morgan could have what she so completely deserved to have. I wasn't so sure about going to a woman's hair salon, but what the heck.

13

Saturday morning was a groundbreaking day for me.

"Good morning princess!" Morgan said as I entered the kitchen.

I kissed her cheek. "Good morning my love. It's Saturday. I hope the haircut doesn't take too long. There's so much for me to do to get things ready for you tonight."

I sat at the table with my juice and cereal. I crossed my high-heeled, stockinged legs and savored the feeling. I smiled at Morgan as she beamed with happiness.

"Daniella, I think you should dress appropriately for the salon treatment today. You should go in looking like a woman, not a man."

"Do you truly think I could? Do you think I'd pass?"

"Of course. You've even been adjusting your voice regularly and your motions and actions are perfect. Besides, a man would look silly coming out of there with long painted fingernails."

"I'm getting my nails done too?"

"Yes. And your dress arrived and I have it hidden for tonight. You'll love it."

I was getting excited thinking about a complete transformation. As good as I looked now, I'd be near perfect after. "Morgan, you're wonderful. Thank you for helping me with this."

She ran her hand through my hair as she bent down and kissed me. "Now, I'll clean the house while you get ready. Take your time and do your best. I'll leave the key to your cage in the bathroom so you can shave down there and make it smooth and pretty."

I finished eating and took my cage off in the shower. The soap made me hard and I shaved it all nice and close. I stroked it a few times then had to stop myself, so I wouldn't feel silly again. I finished showering, put the cage back on, epilated, tweezed my eyebrows, and did my makeup. I left my hair without any hairspray and just fluffed it up with the hair dryer.

I dressed: a denim skirt, some high-heel mules, a V-neck sweater, and jewelry. No stockings, since they were going to do my nails. I needed to get my ears pierced sometime too. The clips were too uncomfortable and kept falling off.

I sprayed perfume all over myself and walked downstairs. Morgan was just finishing cleaning the house. "You look beautiful Daniella. I'll get dressed and we can go."

The salon girls treated me like a queen and three of them worked on me at once. The shag haircut was tremendous and would probably look good in male mode too.

I loved my painted toenails and my new long nailed hands. They made me feel complete.

We seated ourselves in the car. I loved driving in heels and feeling the leather seat on my thighs.

"Daniella, you look fabulous," Morgan said as she took me in while I drove.

"Thanks! I have so much to do before the party."

"Yes you do and so do I. All my men are looking forward to meeting you."

"They know about me?"

"Of course, they know about you. I had to feel them out during their interviews, and I didn't want any of them to give you a hard time, or make you feel bad. They know you're an ex-male in chastity now that has been feminized to the max and is going to watch them and maybe record them, making love to me. I don't think they'll be ready for how beautiful you actually look though. They might hit on you."

"You think so. Hmm. You said all the men. How many are coming tonight?"

"Three or four. I'm not sure if Billy from work is going to make it or not."

"Billy from work?"

"Yes. As it turned out, wearing the keys around my neck introduced me to six other men that understood what it meant. So right now, there are about ten men to chose from at

61

any given time. Tonight, I'll only have three, or four, making love to me."

I drove home lost in the thought of what Morgan had said about the men coming over and them hitting on me. Then I thought of three or four of them with their hands all over her caressing and satisfying her. I throbbed in my cage picturing her in bliss.

What if they hit on me? What would I do? What could I do? Did I care if they did? I wasn't sure. All I knew was there was dinner for six to be purchased and prepared, as well as tables to be set, and primping and getting ready…so much to do!

"Morgan, do you know what they like to eat and drink?"

"Of course. I sent you an email. Steaks would be best, since they all like steak and potatoes. A couple of bottles of bourbon and some cigars would be good. Oh, and a box of Magnum prophylactics."

"Can we stop on the way home so I can buy it all?"

"Of course."

I pulled into the corner drug store and walked in hearing my high-heels as they announced the steps of a sexy woman. I found the Magnums and bought the big box. When I placed them on the counter, the young lady smiled and rang them. "Nice, you're a lucky girl to have a guy that can wear these. Most men can't, they'd just fall off of them." She giggled. "It's so nice when a woman can have a real man isn't it. You're a lucky woman." She bagged them.

"Thanks for saying that."

14

We arrived at home and took a bath. She said I didn't have to help, since we both had so much to get done. I made appetizer plates, set the drink glasses out, and polished the silverware for dinner so we could use the good china with it. I ironed the napkins and folded them in tulips in the wine glasses. Opened the wine and let it breathe.

I seasoned the steaks and cleaned the asparagus so it was ready to steam. Boiled some potatoes and mashed them with butter and sour cream. I set the candelabras up on the dining room table and put a lighter there for later. I put the Magnums in a bowl by the bed and some in a bowl on the coffee table, just in case.

I put fresh flowers on the nightstands by our bed and on the dining room table. I stopped and looked around for anything I missed. I was done. I had an hour and a half to shower and dress. I was a sweaty mess.

I stripped, took a shower, washed and conditioned my hair, and blew it dry. The new shag haircut was incredible the way it framed my face.

I yelled to Morgan. "What color is my dress?"

She yelled back, "It's white. Think bridal. Pink eyeshadow and pink lipstick would be good."

I did my makeup. In the bedroom was Morgan almost finished dressing and she had clothes out for me on the bed. As she put her last phallus-earring in her ear, she saw me in the mirror.

"Oh good sweetie. I have your things out." She turned to me in a short, white, bridal-looking dress with crinoline and a low cut top. The dress had been modified so her nipples protruded from it and the areola showed. She had noose type jewelry on her nipples, making them appear even larger and harder.

"Wow," I said.

She turned and lifted the hem of her dress, showing me her white crotchless panties and white lace-top stockings attached to a white lace garter belt. Five and half inch high-heels with silver ribbons tied on each ankle drew attention to her pretty feet.

Her auburn-red hair was loosely tied back and her makeup, flawless. She winked at me. "Do I look okay?"

"You look incredible." I throbbed in my cage.

"I think if you can be a good girl and control yourself and not release, we should take the cage off so you can wear some crotchless panties and let it be free under the silky lining of your dress." She held up my dress, smiling from ear to ear.

It was a short white bridal outfit with a V-neck, short hem, and crinoline puffing out the skirt - very similar to hers.

I was dying to feel it on. "Oh, thank you, Morgan. It's beautiful. I'll take the cage off and do my best."

"No, not your best. You mustn't orgasm. You mustn't, or you know how you might feel. Maybe if you get over this remorse bullshit from our societal taboos and beliefs, you could come a dozen times tonight, however until that day arrives, you mustn't come tonight. If you can promise me that you can do that without the cage, then you can go free beneath that dress. You can wrap your male parts in the ribbons, bows, and flowers you bought the other day, and make it cute and pretty."

My heart raced. Could I resist releasing? I had to. This was too exciting to pass up. "I can do it."

"Good girl. Now, finish getting ready."

I slid the white silky stockings over my hot pink painted toenails and felt the gossamer thin fabric caress me. I attached them to the garterbelt and looked at myself pulsing free in the air. The white lace bra was a perfect fit and held my cleavage in proper presentation. The heels were like Morgan's - very high - and felt luscious. The dress slipped on and Morgan helped me zip it.

Morgan opened the closet and took out something. It was two bridal veils with hair clips. She slid one in my hair. "There, a virgin bride. So pretty."

Looking in the mirror, she put her veil in her hair. She did look like a bride. It reminded me of when we were married, except back then, she didn't have as sexy a wedding dress.

My bride had become an erotic, sensual, lusting-bride ready to satisfy men and be satisfied. Gorgeous! My decorated and demasculinized remnant of my maleness jumped and leapt under the dress and slid the tip against the satin fabric, making me twitch.

I looked around the room.

"What are you looking for Daniella?"

"A place to put a video camera, if that's okay."

"Of course. I already took care of that. There are three in here so you can get all the angles and edit it into one later if you want. I have a plan for this video to help you get rid of your remorse about all of this. It'll be a reward for you."

"Awesome. Do I need to start them?"

"No, they're already running. They have motion detectors and eight hours worth of memory. There are three downstairs too."

She pointed them out in the bedroom. She came over to me and gingerly kissed my lips. "Ready?"

"Ready."

"Let me decorate down there with my ribbons and flowers and put on some perfume. I'll be right down."

I wrapped and tied myself and it lifted those parts to touch the fabric more frequently, stimulating me with each step. I had to resist the constant teasing this would give me.

My heart raced and pounded in my chest as I made my way down the stairs.

15

We had time for a drink before Morgan's lovers arrived and we both needed it. It was a good nervousness though, because I could see how much Morgan was looking forward to it.

"Don't worry about my men. They promised to treat you with respect."

The doorbell rang. "Go answer it Daniella. I'll be right behind you."

"Oh no, please." I whispered.

"Go."

I clicked daintily to the door and opened it.

"Hi my name's Billy." His hand shot out to shake mine.

"Come in, please. My name is Daniella. Morgan will be right here."

He came in. So, this was the Billy she worked with. He was handsome. About six-foot-two, thick brown wavy hair, and clear smooth skin. Maybe twenty-five or so. He smelled wonderful.

"Mmm, you smell nice."

"Thanks. You do too. And, you're much prettier than I thought you'd be. I could see why you wouldn't want to be a man. Why masquerade as a man when you can look like you do?"

"Why, uh, thanks. Come sit and I'll get you a drink. bourbon, gin, wine, beer,…"

"Gin martini, dirty would be nice. Triple x dirty."

"Please, go sit and I'll get it for you."

The first gorgeous specimen of a man to arrive walked into the great room and I clicked my way into the kitchen, feeling myself twitch with each step from the friction going on under my dress. I made his drink and brought it to him. Morgan was already kneeling before him, consuming him as he sat back on the couch. I put the drink in his hand.

He smiled. "Thanks. This is great. Have a seat." He patted the sofa next to him. I seated myself and crossed my legs, adjusting things under the dress as I did.

I watched my wife devour his huge piece. It was wet and had some of her lipstick around the shaft about half way down. He gently rested his hand on her bridal veil and pumped lightly into her lips. Morgan was looking up into his eyes. The doorbell rang. Morgan's eyes looked over at me while she continued imbibing his manhood.

I stood and answered the door. Tall, dark and handsome. Six-foot-four, or so. Black, silky, slicked back hair and dark olive skin. His hand stuck out to me. His silk

70

pants already revealed what he had. "Manny. You must be Daniella."

I daintily shook his thick hand. "Yes, I am. Come in and have a seat. I'll get you a drink."

"Bourbon, neat please."

The second of four men that would make love to my wife walked confidently into the great room and sat on the love seat. I poured his drink, gave it to him, and then clicked in my heels in my tiny steps, back to the kitchen. I was so nervous. What would I do now, since Morgan had her mouth full of her man, with another one waiting? Soon, three more of them will show up. I couldn't just sit and chat, could I?

My heart was racing as I took a plate of appetizers out to them. I held it for Manny and he took a couple. I placed it on the table next to him. As I was wondering what to do next, Billy put his martini down on the table next to him and held Morgan's head as he grunted and pushed into her mouth with his hips. Morgan struggled to swallow it all, and only missed a little. When she finished licking him clean, she stood and kissed his lips.

"Thanks baby. That was awesome. I promise I'll last for you tonight," he said.

"I hope so." She turned, looked at Manny, and put her arms out to him. "Manny! Unzip that fly baby, you're next." She kneeled before him and started in on him. Billy asked me to sit by him, relax, and have a drink.

"I left it in the kitchen. I'll be right back."

I fetched my martini and sat next to him. He put his arm around me and pulled me close. "You're a pretty girl. Very sexy too. Are you participating tonight, or just helping your wife?"

"Just helping." My face flushed at the thought of participating. Then again, what was helping? Doing what Morgan was doing?

I laid down my limits. "Helping with the food and drinks and things like that. Just serving and helping her out. Watching too. I like to watch her enjoy herself."

"That's good. It's good to see a husband that's willing to bend over backwards for his wife. That's what a real man would do. You went the extra step for her. Especially becoming an ex-male by feminizing yourself like you have." He looked at me up and down. It was like being on display. I nervously smiled a fake smile as best I could. He touched my hair gently, and then my cheek with the back of his hand caressing it.

He nodded his head. I think you're probably better the way you are than as a man. It seems to be your true nature."

I looked at the floor feeling sheepish. "Thanks. I guess."

The doorbell rang, giving me a task to do, which brought me out of my thoughts of what he said and how it was making me feel. "Excuse me." I daintily walked to the door feeling my hips sway lightly and there were two twins about six-feet-tall with blond hair with blue eyes. They were two more very handsome and very cute partners for my wife. They both spoke at the same time.

"Aaron and Allen. Hi." They stuck their hands out.

I shook their hands and led them in. "Drinks?"

"Sure, gin and tonic please," said Aaron, and Allen nodded.

The friction against me under my dress was taking me to the edge as I walked carefully into the kitchen and mixed their drinks. When I came back out, Manny was flooding Morgan's throat. He held her head tight and I knew his meat was down her throat by the way her throat swelled with each thrust into her neck. She was swallowing all of it and she didn't gag. I stood there with the drinks in my hands, watching in awe with everyone else. It was incredible. When he was done grunting and pumping her face, he let go of her head, she popped off with a slurp and a smile.

Everyone applauded.

Morgan stood and wiped her lips with the back of her hand. "Aaron and Allen, hi. Manny, go sit with Billy on the big couch so Allen and Aaron can sit here and I can get things going, so we can drink and eat."

Manny moved and took his drink and Aaron and Allen took his place on the love seat. Morgan kneeled before Allen. They both unzipped their pants and started stroking themselves. Morgan looked at their busy hands and then at me.

"Daniella, do you think you could help me here? It'll be much easier if you could take care of Aaron while I do Allen. If the men don't mind, that is."

Allen and Aaron smiled and Aaron motioned to me to come over. "Come on Daniella, don't be shy. You're gorgeous. Let me put a treat in your mouth baby."

My heart raced as I tried to decide what to do. Morgan was already consuming Allen and I held both their drinks in my hand. I was stuck in place. I couldn't move.

Aaron spoke to me as he rested a hand on Morgan's head. "We can take those drinks from you Daniella." He held a hand out. I handed one to him and gave the other to Allen. Allen had his gorgeous silky rod in his hand, stroking it. It, like the rest, was huge. He winked at me.

Aaron said, "Come here baby. Is this your first time? Don't be afraid. I won't spew in your mouth if you don't want me to. You can just jerk it off if you want. You don't even need to suck it. C'mon, baby. You're hot." He waved me over.

I knelt in front of him. He took my hand and wrapped it around his thick piece. I stroked it and watched how he enjoyed it. It felt so hard, thick, and warm in my hand. He was shaved clean and smelled fresh. He slid closer to the edge of the sofa. I stroked him right before my face. The tip oozed and glistened.

He put his hand gently on the veil on my head. "Such pretty hair. Great hairdo too. Just lick it once. Only if you want to though. Just try it."

I licked the tip and he shuddered. I liked the response, so I did it again. Then again. Then I wrapped my lips around the tip and ran my tongue over it, making him tense all over. I dove onto the shaft with my lips wrapped around it. He held my head gently.

"That a girl. Good girl. That feels so nice."

I sucked and licked his shaft, and tugged on his shaved globes with my hands. I loved the way he responded to me. It tasted and smelled like some exotic treat. I wanted him to release for me. No. I NEEDED to have him release for me so I knew how sexy I truly was. My feminized ego required it.

I bobbed my head up and down quickly and Aaron made the job easier by holding my head and pumping into my face instead. I knew he was ready and I looked up at him. When he saw my eyes, he filled my mouth with one gush after another. I counted and swallowed each gush - nine, full, thick, creamy loads that tasted awesome. Not like mine did after I messed my cage and Morgan fed it to me. It must have been my arousal that made it so good. I leaked some cream under my skirt; even so, I valiantly resisted the temptation to let it go.

Aaron held my face, leaned down, and kissed my lips. "Thanks. You were incredible. Are you okay doll?"

I smile and licked my lips. "That was fun. I do need to fix my lipstick though, don't I?"

"Go right ahead baby. You're gorgeous."

I proudly stepped my way in dainty steps to the bathroom, and freshened up my lipstick.

Evidently, Morgan had just finished with Allen.

"Nice job Daniella. Your first SUCK-cess," She yelled to me.

The group applauded as I came out.

"Thanks. It was great. I'm so hot though. I need to cool off outside for a while and have my drink."

I took my martini out to the porch to get some air and cool down. Stepping onto the porch, I felt the cool breeze blow up my dress and against my oozing thing. My breasts felt luscious against my chest. I sipped my martini, swallowed the last of Aaron's cream in my mouth, and licked it off my gums. I was strangely proud to have it to savor.

I just brought a gorgeous man to a pinnacle of pleasure while I was dressed as a woman, and all the men thought I was gorgeous. What a night this was starting out to be. I swayed my hips and felt myself slipping under the dress as I sipped my martini.

Oh well, enough lingering. I needed to get dinner going for my wife and her four new lovers.

16

The night continued as it started. A feast for all. Morgan had all four of them as I watched her in our bed. Huge hands caressed and delighted her. Every position she was in and each man seemed to top the first in the way her pleasure grew. They all made passionate love to her and at times, all at once.

Her entire body was a pallet for them to paint pleasure on with their bodies and hands. The way her body writhed and twitched. How her eyes rolled in her head. The sometimes moaning, sometimes whimpering, sometimes screaming, her voice helped emphasize what a fantastic thing I had given her.

I was able to capture her gratification intimately and at close range on one of the video cameras I took down and hand carried. The attention I gave the camera kept me busy and kept me from releasing. I was able then to savor the bliss on her face throughout the process as one gorgeous man after another filled her, released in her, and thoroughly satisfied her, giving her orgasm after rolling orgasm. I was the luckiest man in the world to have her.

I ate breakfast as Morgan slept in, and I made myself as beautiful as I could. I wore a pinstriped, short, skirt-suit and black, spiked, high-heel pumps. My hair was gelled in the new shag in a new style I came up with.

Morgan held the counter as she came into the kitchen. Her eyes were droopy.

"Can someone have a sex overdose? My God. I hardly drank anything, yet my body feels like shit." She kissed my cheek. "You, however look lovely. How are you?"

"I'm great. You should be sore. All the contorting and pounding you had. You take a rest today and I'll clean up, I'll wash the sheets, make the bed, and clean up the party-mess down here. You can take a bath and soak those aches and pains away."

"You might want to wash my dress." She poured a coffee and stood straddle-legged by the counter.

"I will. I need to wash mine too."

I looked at her apologetically with my head down and eyes peeking up.

I started to talk quickly to let her know how bad I was. "I couldn't hold it in inside anymore. Sorry. I tried not to. I tried so hard. The excitement of watching you made love to for so long, and then, and then, oh my God, I mean, when the last one pumped and finished in you, I spurted all under my dress without touching myself. My knees wobbled and I nearly fell down it was so good! I'm so sorry."

"That's okay princess. Did you have any remorse?"

"Other than disappointing you that I did that, no. It seemed so natural to be doing what we did and for me to be the way I was. I think stimulating Aaron to release in my mouth helped me see what it's like to give and receive pleasure, no matter how you act or dress. I never did that to a man and before I wouldn't have even imagined wanting to do that. It made him so happy though, and by doing that, it made me happy that I could do it so well. It was so exciting to get him to react to me like that."

I looked at the floor feeling a bit embarrassed at what I just told my wife.

I looked back up at her. "I guess you were right. It was all societal conditioning. Now, the experiential learning has taught me that this is all good. No one is getting hurt. Everyone is having safe, adult fun. Our marriage is stronger than ever. What could be better?"

Morgan smiled her bright green eyes and wobbled over to me. She kissed me on the lips. "I love you."

"I love you too." I was so relieved to hear that.

I started to talk quickly again. "How about after I get everything cleaned up and you rest, I make a nice dinner for us and we watch a movie, cuddling on the couch? Dressed nicely, of course if that's okay. I'll get your clothes ready and give you a bath." I laughed.

I moved in front of her and knelt down so I could look up at her and spoke quickly and excitedly while I held my palms together as if in prayer. "Maybe we can do what we used to do afterwards. You know. I could play the role of a man, but in a dress of course."

Morgan smiled and nodded her head looking down at me as she patted my head like a teacher to a student. "There's nothing more that I would like than to have you do that. It's still the best feeling in the world having someone you love do that. Especially now that you know who you are, and what's good."

Morgan continued, "Let's cuddle and watch an old movie and then, if you don't mind, you fill me where four other men did last night, while I wear the same dress and you wear the same dress you watched them in. If there's no remorse there, there'll never be any. That shouldn't take but a moment and afterwards, the cage goes back on for a few weeks. This can be your reward night. I won't count your little accidental spurting last night."

"That sounds wonderful honey." I stood and adjusted my skirt, feeling my uncaged, unencumbered, and dripping rod slip against the fabric. I looked into the little mirror on the wall and adjusted my hair. "I'll need to get pierced ears soon. Do you think I could get away with two in each ear and still wear men's' clothes?"

"Of course dear. No one will care. No one will know. Just us and my lovers."

I turned and clicked over to her. I kissed her on her lips gently so as not to mess my lipstick. "Can I make you breakfast or should I run the tub. I need to get this place cleaned up and you're in my way."

"Run the tub. Please. I'll stay out of your way."

"Thanks honey. Let me get things ready for you."

If you enjoyed this book, please leave a review and tell a friend. Thanks.

Other books by Barbara Deloto and Thomas Newgen can be found at:

http://www.ShapeShifterBook.com

Printed in Great Britain
by Amazon

78745651R00050